MW01716385

A REVIEW TO DIE FOR

BOOK 3 OF THE KAREN CARTER SERIES

R.E. SARGENT

SINISTER SMILE PRESS

A REVIEW TO DIE FOR

Published by Sinister Smile Press, LLC
P.O. Box 637
Newberg, OR 97132

Copyright © 2019 by R.E. Sargent

All rights reserved. This book or any portion thereof may not be reproduced or used in any manner whatsoever without the express written permission of the publisher, except for the use of brief quotations in a book review.

This is a work of fiction. Names, characters, businesses, places, events, and incidents are either the products of the author's imagination or used in a fictitious manner. Any resemblance to actual persons, living or dead, or actual events is purely coincidental.

Printed in the United States of America

Trade Paperback ISBN – 978-1-953112-61-3

www.sinistersmilepress.com

contents

For My Readers–

One-Star Review and *Becoming Karen Carter* were never meant to be a series. I wrote them and moved on to other projects. Thanks to your reviews and messages, Karen Carter lives on in this third installment. I'll keep the series going as long as the fans want more. Keep the feedback coming and thank you!

And for Miranda–

I can't thank you enough for your reviews—the ones in real life and the fictional review you wrote in this installment of the series. I, for one, am glad I wasn't on the receiving end of *that* scorcher! Also, thanks for volunteering to be killed in this book—I had fun doing it!

And for Steven–

Thanks for making the new covers for this series. You nailed it! (Pun intended.) Thank you also for your contributions to this novelette. I'm grateful!

And for RJ–

Thanks for your input with this novelette. Your suggestion was on-point. I appreciate it!

chapter one

Jessica Nichols packed the final box in her bedroom and taped the flaps shut. It had been five months since she started living in Manhattan full-time—ever since Lana Brooks had so easily given up the high-rise apartment where Jessica now resided.

Okay, so it hadn't been that easy. The struggle was intense and Lana put up a huge fight, Jessica finding herself on the receiving end of a knife. She was hurt badly enough that she could have died, but what mattered most was that Jessica came out the victor.

Exhausted from her packing activities, Jessica grabbed a bottle of iced tea out of the refrigerator and went out to her back patio. It was the last time she would enjoy this little slice of California paradise. Her thirst seemingly unquenchable, she downed half of the drink in one series of chugs.

Her thoughts turned to whom she had become. It wasn't long ago that she lived here in this house, furiously trying to get noticed in the publishing world, as she eked out manuscript after manuscript. Her means of survival were the proceeds from the latest lawsuit she had filed after antagonizing a coworker so badly that it resulted in Jessica being attacked.

Then there was the murder. As a writer, Jessica was also a voracious reader and she binge-read everything she could find by the author Karen Carter. That adoration grew into an obsession, which quickly turned to jealousy. It was when Jessica realized that Karen Carter—which was really the pseudonym of a woman by the name of Lana Brooks—was killing off readers that left shitty reviews of her books, Jessica decided two could play at that game. If Lana Brooks could kill to get what she wanted, so could Jessica.

On that fateful night five months ago, Jessica gained access to Lana's apartment and lay in wait for her, attacking her when she arrived home from her latest murder spree.

When Lana perished, Jessica took over Lana's life: her finances, her apartment and her writing career. Jessica Nichols was the new Karen Carter.

Now, Jessica was back in her California home in the City of Orange, loading up the last of her personal items to take back with her. The moving truck was coming in an hour to pick up the boxes, but the furniture and the remainder of the items were to be picked up by the Salvation Army the following day. The real estate agent that lived down the street had listed the house a few hours prior. She expected a quick sale. The apartment overlooking the city had everything she needed.

She reflected again on how desperate she had become. How dangerous. As hard as she tried, she was unable to fathom that she had actually taken a life. Was it justified since Lana Brooks was also a killer? Was the eye-for-an-eye mentality a valid one? It really didn't matter how she tried to justify it. She knew deep down in her heart that she would kill again. She had enjoyed it. It was only a matter of time before it happened a second time.

Three months after Jessica had taken over the apartment and started submitting books as Karen Carter—using both Lana's finished manuscripts as well as her own—she came across her first mean-spirited one-star review. To make matters worse, it was from a popular online reviewer that had a huge following. Jessica remembered how her vision had turned red and she could think of nothing else. A pit in the deepest part of her stomach opened up and she felt as if the room were spinning out of control. The hundreds of rejection letters from her past crept into her brain—the voices telling her that she was not good enough; would never be good enough. It was another taste of rejection and she was not equipped to deal with it.

That night, Jessica had opened up the desk drawer where Lana Brooks kept all her login instructions to gain access to Amazon's customer information. She logged in, surprised that even as Lana Brooks lay in pieces at the bottom of the nearest landfill, the access information still worked. Jessica knew that Lana Brooks had killed many of her one-star reviewers. She now understood why. She decided she would take a page out of Lana's book—pun intended—and regulate the situation. It's who she had become. She would carry on in the tradition of the one who built the Karen Carter name before her. As she sat at the desk, Jessica worked her way through the instructions until she had the reviewer's name and address on the screen in front of her. This was her next victim. She absolutely would not let this reviewer get away with diminishing Karen Carter's work and tarnishing her good name, even if it wasn't her own.

Now, turning her focus back to the task at hand in California, Jessica took another big gulp of her tea and went back inside. Two months had passed since that day—the day Jessica had vowed to kill the person that had left her that shitty review—yet she still failed to act. She had the reviewer's name. She had her address. She wondered if there was something left of her defunct moral code that was pushing back inside her brain. She knew it wasn't self-control. That part of her wanted to kill the bitch and make it hurt.

The next day, the Salvation Army workers came and removed all the rest of the items from the house. With her personal items on the truck to Manhattan, her house listed, her car sold—she had taken it to a dealer for a cash offer—Jessica took one last look around. A sadness took over as she thought about leaving the house behind, but she knew she had bigger and better things to do and keeping both places on opposite ends of the United States didn't make any sense to her. At least not at this stage in her life.

With one final glance, Jessica pulled the door shut behind her, got in the rental car and drove to John Wayne airport. When she made it to her gate, she pulled out her laptop and started writing, trying to kill the two-hour wait before the plane boarded.

Jessica loved her new laptop, which was actually Lana's old one. When she had taken over Lana's life, she found it was easy to do everything she needed to since most of Lana's passwords were stored in the computer. That and the fact that it was a top-of-the-line MacBook Pro worked out well for her.

Jessica continued to work on her latest novel as she waited to board. She had just finished the last of the novels Lana had been working on and submitted them to the publisher. The publisher had two novels mostly written by Lana waiting to be released. Jessica had pitched the new series she had been working on for years and it was accepted, which she expected. One of those titles had been released already and the next one would release in a few months thereafter, establishing a release cadence of twice per year for the new series and twice a year for Lana's old series. That would equate to four releases a year. Aggressive, but manageable.

The flight was uneventful as she knew it would be. Since becoming Karen Carter—and acquiring her small fortune in the process—Jessica flew only first class and always received impeccable service. Back at LaGuardia, she ordered an Uber and waited for it to arrive. Her thoughts turned toward the apartment and the brutal struggle from five months earlier.

Searching the deepest pit of her soul, she tried to find any remorse that resided there, waiting to be recognized. Nothing. Jessica decided then she was going to hell. *Well I might as well enjoy the ride then*, she thought.

Back in her Manhattan apartment, Jessica poured herself a drink and went out on the balcony, staring at the Manhattan skyline. While there were certain things that she loved about her California home, there was no better view than the one she had in this apartment. She couldn't get enough of it.

As the air became chilly, Jessica went inside and locked the French doors. She sat down at the bar counter and opened up her laptop. Bringing up the reviews on her last published book, she filtered by number of stars and brought the review up one more time—the review that had her mind reeling with murderous thoughts.

Just wait, it gets worse!

By Miranda Reads

Oh, good lawd. Not this again.

We follow the brilliant Bethany Summers. She's got brains, she's got brawn, she's got size triple D's...well, you get the point. Essentially, if her name wasn't Mary Sue, then I'm not Miranda Reads.

Bethany, focusing on her assets, spends the first quarter of the book reminiscing about how lucky she is. She owns a thriving antique store (in a town with population 500 and NO tourist trade? HOW?). She's dating Mr. Hunky McHunkerson (rich and devilishly handsome—what are the odds!). And just when things look bleakest, a mysterious estate sale pops up—just in the nick of time! Oh, the coincidences!

However, after she receives the mystery items, her shop experiences three break-ins, with the thief in the third one making off with an unopened chest from the estate sale—a chest that (for some poorly defined reason) must be kept out of enemy hands…or else.

So, as many of you know, I am ***NOT*** *a big Karen Carter fan.*

I just can't really see the appeal—her Southern Sins standalone made me hurl, the Rambunctious Daze series was as interesting as drywall and Words Never Lie was comedically cringey.

And yet. Here I am. At Carter's doorstep. Again.

Why?

*Because **SOMEONE** has to take the bullet for you all.*

***SOMEONE** needs to read and review it solely so you don't have to waste your precious time.*

And I volunteer. I volunteer as tribute to the world of literary sins.

And what a sinful world this was.

Carter violated the BIG THREE—characters, plot and dialogue—so completely and thoroughly that this book really should be considered a work of art.

Characters—aka, is that you, again?

Every character was Bethany—I'm serious.

There literally was nothing to distinguish Bethany from McHunkerson from the stranger with a secret. Their tone, inflection and word choice overlapped 110%.

IF I'm going to shell out $15.99 (FOR A PAPERBACK, MIND YOU) the author better damn well put forth some effort.

P.S. – There was literally no need for every character to sashay, strut, glide, prance or whatever synonym your thesaurus vomited up on you. It's called walking. W-A-L-K-I-N-G.

The Plot—aka started from the bottom, now we're here...still at the bottom.

The story had more plotholes than my city has potholes.

Who lets their store get robbed THREE times without installing a security system?

How did Bethany manage to change in front of an open window with a creeper across the street—FIVE times in one book?

How does the sheriff, the deputy, assistant what's-his-face and the secretary ALL have the same week off just when a string of murderers roll into town?

I get that Carter wants a one-woman powerhouse of a character, but how hard is it for her to at least TRY?

Dialogue—aka that signature cringe.

Ahhh, it just wouldn't be Carter without the cringe-factor.

Every conversation, from that constant loose upper button on Bethany's blouse, to the faintly Scottish lilt from McHunkerson (who…was born and raised in the US) just hit me with that spine-tingling, cringe factor.

It was stilted, the innuendo was off the charts and if I ever heard anyone talk like that in real life, I think I'd just run the other direction.

Overall—aka now what?

In all honesty, it is up to you whether or not you will pick this book up (did I mention $15.99 for a PAPERBACK? Oh, I did? Good).

One thing's for certain—I will read her next book. And I will review it. And I know I'm going to hate it.

P.S. – Just a reviewer's note—the sheer irony of "Busty Bethany" having to protect her "chest" throughout...not among Carter's better moments.

Jessica inhaled sharply as the words stung deep once again. She tried not to let it bother her knowing that the review was actually for a book that Lana had penned, but her mind didn't work that way. Karen Carter was now *her* pen name. It was *her* brand. When someone trashed her name, they trashed her future. She needed to deal with it, but apprehension took over once again as it had a couple of months prior. Closing the laptop, Jessica went into the bedroom, slipped out of her clothes and got ready for bed. A good night's sleep would put her in a better frame of mind.

At least she hoped so.

chapter **two**

The blinding sun slipping through the cracks in the blinds caused Jessica to awake. The apartment seemed too warm for the April morning and she rolled over and used the remote to flip on the ceiling fan. In seconds, a cold chill racked her body around the same time she noticed her clothes were damp. Peeling back the covers, the sheets revealed more clues. They were soaked. Jessica had been sweating during her slumber.

Disgusted with the way her damp nightie clung to her, Jessica pulled it over her head, stripped off the bedsheets and threw them all in the washer, starting the load before she hopped in the shower.

After she dried off, she wrapped the towel around her and went to the bathroom mirror to brush her hair. The haunting face that stared back worried her.

She had dark circles under her eyes that detracted from her high cheekbones. Her silky, blonde hair hung past her shoulders but didn't do anything to help minimize the look of exhaustion. She studied her body in the mirror. Still firm. The pink scar from the knife wound caught her attention and she touched it, running her fingertip over the raised flesh.

I gave everything to be here.

Jessica pushed her hair back behind her shoulders and touched the dark skin under her left eye. It felt puffy to her touch.

No one is going to screw with my life.

Jessica selected concealer from the array of makeup in the drawer and applied it under both eyes.

After getting dressed, she entered her library and opened up her laptop once again. She brought the review from two months prior up on the screen. Angst filled her heart as she read the headline over and over.

Just wait, it gets worse!

Jessica remembered the nightmare she'd been having that had caused her to drench the bed in sweat. In the dream, she had heard a voice outside—calling, beckoning. In the dream, she went out on the balcony and looked down, only to see a person standing on the sidewalk all the way down at ground level. He stared directly at her. As she asked him what he was doing, he called to her, telling her how terrible of an author she was. She yelled back—even flipped him off—but then others joined him. One person turned to two. Two turned to five. Five to ten and then the street and sidewalk were completely covered with people, yelling and screaming about how bad she was, how terrible her books were, how she was a piece of crap.

Unable to think of anything else, Jessica slid out the drawer that contained the contact information of the reviewer. She pulled out the single sheet of paper and studied it. Florida. Her thoughts turned toward booking a trip there. What would she do when she got there? How could she pull something like this off without getting caught?

Her thoughts turned to Lana and the struggle they had in the master bedroom. She had managed to pull off that murder and no one was any wiser. She could certainly pull off the murder of some book reviewer that wanted to screw with her livelihood.

Unsure of herself, Jessica pulled up the website Lana had used to gather more information on people. She entered Miranda Read's full name—courtesy of Amazon—into the search field and narrowed it down to an address in Tampa, Florida. While the system searched millions of online records, Jessica went into the kitchen and started a cup of coffee.

Back at her desk, she scoured the results. Miranda was twenty-six years old. Married to the store manager of a local Jiffy Lube. Office Manager at a construction company. No kids. The home address looked like an apartment complex.

Jessica crumpled the piece of paper in a ball and threw it in the trash.

What the hell am I even thinking? she wondered.

She leaned back in her desk chair with her fingers interlaced behind her head, stretching out her back.

I can't believe I'm willing to jeopardize everything I have over a stupid review!

Jessica grabbed her coffee cup and went into the kitchen, grabbing some granola out of the pantry. Pouring herself a bowl, she added milk and sat at the table, watching the window washers work their way down the building across from her. She tried to calm her anxiety, knowing it would drive her to make stupid decisions. There was no way she could kill someone and risk everything. There was nothing to be gained by doing so. Instead, she had everything to lose.

Hoping to distract herself from the recurring vision of the review, Jessica cleaned up after herself and took the elevators down to the lobby. Outside, the doorman hailed her a cab and she asked the driver to take her to Saks Fifth Avenue. A little shopping therapy was in order.

After dropping a couple of thousand dollars at Saks, Jessica was hoping to feel better, but the review was still nagging at her, begging her to take action.

She grabbed another cab to Bloomingdales and after a couple of hours there, hopped another one to The Gilded Grape for a bottle of wine, before heading back to the apartment building.

With the sun setting low in the sky, Jessica decided to cook a nice meal of braised pork loin. It had been a while since she cooked anything fancy and she knew it would pair well with the bottle of wine she picked up earlier. She popped the cork and poured a glass which she savored while cooking.

While the tasks in front of her should have pulled her thoughts away from the review, nothing was working.

She must die.

"NO! I'm not going to kill her!" she yelled, to no one in particular.

You must!

Jessica grunted and slammed the pan down on the stove. She was weary from having to wrestle with her thoughts. She was in control, damnit. Her mind needed to listen to what she had to say and back the hell off.

Later, after dinner was ready, she dished the food onto her plate and went out on the balcony to eat. The fresh air and the people behind the windows of the surrounding buildings helped pull her mind away from things and she started to relax. The third glass of wine didn't hurt either.

When she finally brought her plate inside, she put it in the sink and put away the leftovers. Not feeling like doing dishes, yet unable to leave a mess for the next day, Jessica rinsed everything and loaded the dishwasher. Finished in the kitchen for the night, she shut off the lights and only left the side lamps surrounding the couch on as she went to the bedroom to throw on a pair of sweats, before retiring to the library.

At her desk, Jessica brought up the latest manuscript she was working on and tried to type. She was not feeling creative and each time she would type a paragraph, she'd re-read it and hit the backspace key. While she lived to write, it didn't always come easy. She tried to concentrate on the story, yet continued to be distracted.

Her mind started to reflect on negative thoughts.

Just wait, it gets worse!

"Son-of-a-bitch!" she yelled, pounding the desk. "Fine! You win."

Jessica reached into the trash can and pulled out the crumpled-up piece of paper, smoothing it on the desk. She knew she wouldn't be able to concentrate again until she took care of this problem. It looked like Jessica was going to Tampa, Florida.

chapter three

Jessica punched the code into the door and the lock popped open. She pushed her way inside with her suitcase and shut the door behind her. Looking around, she was pleased that the pictures on the vacation rental site were representative of the space's true condition. Looking forward to her week away, she found the bedroom and began unpacking.

Knowing nothing about this Miranda lady, she knew she would have to scope out the situation before making her move. As much as she was conflicted on what she was about to do, she knew she had to get it done in order to move forward in life. That meant she couldn't be stupid, and she definitely couldn't get caught.

The vacation rental she booked was a one-bedroom condo that was on the bay; her balcony overlooked the water. Her first inclination was to stay at a hotel, but this option afforded her more privacy and she could come and go without showing up on hotel camera systems. She was also happy that she could write from this home. Just being in the place where she knew she was going to take care of a problem, she hoped the words would flow. She would definitely take advantage of the time and location when she wasn't busy tailing Miranda.

As much as she wanted to rent a luxury car, she kept it simple—a gray Nissan Altima that did not stand out in any way. She would start her work in the morning.

Being as it was late afternoon, Jessica wanted to eat and relax for the rest of the evening. She looked at the amenities that were listed in the property binder and noticed there was a restaurant within walking distance. Calling the number, she inquired about ordering something to go and was pleased when she found out she could pick up her meal in twenty minutes.

The walk to the restaurant was uneventful and Jessica realized that she was extremely relaxed now that she was in Tampa. Unsure whether it was the vacation-like setting, or the impending murder that was relaxing her, she paid for the food and walked back to the condo. She caught a couple male passersby checking her out as she passed and she smiled. It had been a really long time since she had any fun with a man. Actually, ever since she was assaulted by her boss all those years ago, she had remained single. Maybe on this vacation, she could let loose a little. It would be on her terms if it happened at all.

Back at the condo, she ate while watching the bay and relaxed in one of the chaise lounges that were provided. She had never lived with a water view before and she could get used to this. Maybe one day, she would buy a vacation home in Malibu and live there during the winter. The thought brought a smile to her face.

Later that evening, when the sun slipped away and the water was cast in shadows, she changed into a pair of shorts and a camisole and propped herself up in bed, returning to her manuscript. The words flowed and she found that within two hours, she had written three-thousand words. Looking at the time, she decided to call it a night, shutting down the computer and switching off the light. She would be getting up early the next morning.

Dressed in black jeans and a gray t-shirt, Jessica locked the door behind her and made her way to her rental car. It was early and the sun had barely cast a small bit of light into the morning sky. She wanted to make sure she was early to ensure she didn't miss Miranda.

Twenty minutes later, Jessica found the address and pulled into the apartment complex, looking at the numbers on the sides of the buildings to find the right one. It was halfway around the complex and as soon as she saw it, she parked in an unmarked spot. From her vantage point, she could see the entryways to the apartments on the lower level and the staircases to the upstairs units, but she had no idea which apartment was theirs. Looking around and not noticing any movement, she got out of the Altima and walked over to the nearest apartments, getting closer to the doors to read the numbers. The first two apartments were close, but a few numbers off. Jessica walked down the sidewalk to the next set of doors and found she was headed in the right direction, but she still was not at the right door. One more set of doors down, she found the right one. It was the downstairs apartment on the left.

Slipping back to her car, Jessica moved it to another spot that gave her a direct vantage point to keep an eye on the apartment door, but also kept her out of the main view of the tenants. Now it was just a waiting game.

Around a quarter till seven, Jessica sensed movement and watched carefully. A man dressed in a brown uniform exited the apartment and climbed in a nearby Toyota truck. Jessica made a note of the color and license plate number and watched as he pulled to the street and headed north.

Pleased that the husband left for work first, Jessica started playing out scenarios in her head on how she would get to Miranda. Maybe she could break into the apartment as soon as the man was gone. It could be risky and there might be witnesses. Rather than do anything rash, she decided to wait, observe, and get more information.

Fifteen minutes later, the person that Jessica assumed was Miranda came out of the apartment and locked the door behind her. Jessica eyed her, taking in the details. She appeared to be around five-foot ten and had brown hair with blonde streaks that went halfway down her back. Jessica admired her thin waist and curvy hips even if she despised the person inside. Even in jeans and the unremarkable button-up shirt that Miranda wore, Jessica could tell she was well put together. Just another example of a hot bitch thinking she was better than everyone else.

Looking at her watch, Jessica realized that the two had left the apartment within fifteen minutes of each other. That would most likely mean they got up together and got ready together. Taking care of her at the apartment would not be an option—at least before work.

Jessica started the car and kept Miranda in sight as she pulled onto the street. Keeping her distance, she followed. When they got on the main road, she tried to keep a couple of cars between them as she followed to wherever they were going, which she assumed was Miranda's work. After twenty-five minutes, Miranda turned into a parking lot that was in an industrial area. Jessica continued down the street and turned around, driving back to the lot slowly. As she drove by it for the second time, she saw Miranda's car parked in front of the building and Miranda was walking inside. The sign on the front window boasted "Haskin's Construction." Miranda was indeed at work.

Jessica checked the time and made a note of when

Miranda arrived. She would need to know her schedule to best determine when to strike.

A mile down the road, Jessica pulled off into a shopping center parking lot, parked and pulled out her phone. She looked up Haskin's Construction and found the company website. They were open until five p.m. Back on the road, Jessica drove back by the construction company and at the last minute, decided to pull into the parking lot. The property held the single business which consisted of an office-type building up front and a huge attached metal building behind it. It looked like more of a warehouse than anything and the side of the building had a half-dozen roll-up doors imbedded into it.

Jessica parked her rental car. While she didn't really want to meet the intended victim, she wanted to go inside and learn a little more about the layout as well as how many people worked there. There were way too many potential witnesses at the apartment complex.

As she walked to the front door—a flimsy story for why she was here floating around in the back of her mind—she noticed a couple of vans that were parked on the side, behind a gate, right across from the roll-up doors. Taking a deep breath, anxiety creeping into her demeanor, Jessica threw on her sweetest smile, pulled open the door and stepped inside.

In the lobby area, she saw a few chairs and a counter. Back behind the counter and to the right were a line of offices with windows that overlooked the common area of the office building. To the left, there were a few desks sitting out in the open. Glancing over just as the person sitting at the nearest desk looked at her, Jessica locked eyes with Miranda.

A smile flashed over Miranda's face. "Hi! How can I help you?" She got up from her desk and came to the counter. Jessica realized just how tall she was when she approached, and then there were those eyes —they looked almost black in the florescent lighting.

Jessica smiled back. "Hi. My husband and I are thinking about remodeling our home and are searching for the right contractor to do the job. Do you guys do that sort of thing here?"

"Absolutely! We do all kinds of construction from residential new builds, remodels and repairs to commercial work as well." She held out her hand. "I'm Miranda, the office manager. And you are?"

Jessica shook her hand. "I'm Carrie."

"Nice to meet you, Carrie. What exactly are you and your husband wanting to get done?"

"Pretty much an upgrade of the entire house.

New paint, modern kitchen and bathrooms, new fixtures and appliances. New flooring as well."

"That sounds fantastic. It's always nice to live in an almost new home. We do all of that. Did you want to set up an appointment for one of our estimators to come out, check out the scope of work and get you some pricing?"

"Tell me a little bit about your company first. My husband asked me to check into three different companies and he wants to chat before we commit to having anyone out at the house."

"Sure thing. We are a family-owned company and have been in business eighteen years. We have approximately thirty people working here including myself, an architect, a designer, the bosses and the teams. We typically are working on as many as ten projects at a time depending on size, but when we have bigger projects going, we tend to have less happening at one time. I run the office and the others come and go as they please."

"Seems lonely here working all by yourself," Jessica baited.

"It's not so bad. The workers usually stop in to get their vans in the morning before I get here. They start fairly early. The others are out in the field more than they are here. I enjoy the quiet when the phone isn't ringing. When it's slow, I get to listen to an audiobook here and there as well. It's the perfect job!"

"Well, a cute little thing like yourself shouldn't be all alone," Jessica told her.

Miranda blushed. "Well that just made my day, Hun! Thank you!"

"Welcome! Anyway, do they do good work here?"

"We're one of the best in town. Check out our reviews online. You'll see we get five stars from most of our customers."

"Good to know," Jessica told her, trying to stop her mouth from saying what she knew she was about to. It slipped out before she could control it. "Does your company get many one-star reviews?"

"Only one time," Miranda confessed. "It was really just some jerk that wanted a discount on the work we did. When he didn't get it, he left a bad review."

"What a dick move, leaving you a review like that."

"I couldn't have said it better. The owners were pretty pissed about it. I thought my boss was going to kill him!" Miranda laughed, her silky hair bouncing around as she flashed a perfect set of teeth. Jessica joined in, the irony more than she could handle.

Jessica reached over and took a business card from

the holder. “Let me talk to my husband this afternoon and I’ll get back to you, Miranda. How late are you usually here?”

“Well the office is technically open until five p.m. I try to leave soon after that. Let me know if you or your husband have any questions about anything. That number on the card will reach me directly.”

“I will let you know.” Jessica winked. “I’m sure I’ll be seeing you again.”

“I look forward to it,” Miranda told her.

Jessica grinned. “Me too.” *You have no idea*, she thought.

chapter **four**

Back at the vacation rental, Jessica poured herself a mixed drink. She had stopped at the store on the way back to get a few things for the condo. A bottle of Jim Beam and a two-liter of Coke were part of her purchases. She needed to get a little drunk to prepare for the next day.

As Jessica tried to come up with a plan to take care of the business she was in town for, doubt kept creeping in. She hadn't expected Miranda to be so sweet. She had so badly wanted her to be a complete bitch. At least killing her would have been easier that way.

As she considered hopping on a plane the next day and heading home, she struggled with that plan. Sure, Miranda *seemed* nice, but wasn't she also the one that had left the scathing one-star review for Jessica's novel? Sure, she played nice when she was at her place of employment, but how nice could she truly be? It had to be an act.

Pouring her third drink, Jessica felt conflicted as her mind raged against itself. One side told her she could not kill poor, sweet, Miranda—that it had all been one huge mistake. The other side told her she would never be truly happy or productive until she took care of this distraction in the only manner that made sense. Miranda had to die as planned.

Convinced she needed to carry out the actions she had flown into town to do, Jessica started formulating a plan in her mind. By the time half the bottle was gone, she was so shitfaced that she couldn't even concentrate on what was going on around her, let alone in her mind. A sudden exhaustion took over and she set her glass down on the coffee table, lay her head on the arm of the couch and passed out.

In the morning, Jessica was woken by loud voices outside. Confused, she tried to clear her head, wondering why she was on the couch. She became aware of the dull pressure in her head as well as her screaming bladder and as she stumbled off the couch and slipped into the bathroom, she left the light off to save her throbbing head. She sat on the toilet and tried to clear her thoughts, but everything was fuzzy. She finally realized she had most likely missed her window of opportunity with Miranda, muttered a few profanities under her breath and when she was finished, she flushed and washed up, splashing cold water on her face in the process.

In the dining room, she found her purse on the table and dumped all the contents out, trying to find her Ibuprofen. As she dug around through the pile of junk, her impatience grew, but finally, she found the small bottle and shook four out, slamming them into her mouth and heading to the sink where she cupped the cool liquid into her hands and flushed the pills down her gullet.

The vertical blinds covering the sliding glass door that led to the patio danced around as the slats caught the current from the living room ceiling fan. The sharp slivers of light fired through the room in random patterns assaulting her tortured eyes. There would be nothing happening today. Jessica stumbled into the bedroom, threw the covers back and climbed in, pulling them up over her, closing her eyes and powering through the headache that seemed to only get worse. Within fifteen minutes, the Ibuprofen kicked in and she was asleep.

Jessica awoke again, this time by the urging of her stomach. The room was dark and based upon the lack of light filtering through the blinds, she guessed it was nighttime. She had blown her opportunity by getting drunk. Stupid move.

Jessica stumbled into the kitchen to scrape up something to eat. She tried to collect her thoughts as she ate a sandwich and followed it with some of the coke that was left over from her bender.

Jessica had never been one to be weak. That's how life pulled you under the tires. She had come to Tampa for a reason and she was going to carry it out. Even though that bitch Miranda was playing all nice and shit, Jessica had to see through it. Deep down, Miranda was an evil internet bully that loved to trash other people for her own amusement. Most of the reviews she left were testament to that. At work, she *had* to be nice. The Miranda that Jessica had met at the construction company was merely a masked version of the real thing. It was a ruse.

As the food tore away at her hunger, she decided

she would pay Miranda a visit the next day. If her timing was right, she would take care of business.

The next morning when Jessica got up, she felt better than she had the night before. Her headache had returned before she went back to bed and she ended up popping more ibuprofen to eat away at the throbbing pain that attacked her.

Showered and dressed, Jessica got into her car and drove to the industrial park that housed the construction business. There were no customers as she had experienced before. She parked in front of the building and went inside.

Miranda looked up from her desk. "Hey, Sweetie, welcome back!"

Sweetie? Jessica thought. *No! I'm not going to let her throw me off my game by calling me Sweetie.* "Good to see you again. Are you super busy?"

"Not too busy for you. What brings you by?"

"My husband, Cory, liked what I told him about you guys. He wanted me to check into your company a little more before we asked for a bid. I figured why not hear it straight from my friend Miranda's mouth. Gives me a great excuse to come see you and maybe even learn more about the business."

Miranda appeared to be blushing a bit and Jessica wondered if Miranda thought she was flirting with her. Whatever it took to throw her off her game, Jessica was going to do it.

"So, what else do you want to know?" Miranda asked, her face breaking out in a huge smile.

"I think my husband is mostly worried about quality."

"I get it. Did you check out our reviews?"

"Only one so far. I'll check out the rest soon."

"Well they do say a lot about our company."

"This place really looks amazing," Jessica baited, looking around. "Can you give me a tour and show me a little behind the scenes?"

Miranda hesitated. Finally, she spoke. "Our insurance company doesn't like customers in our work areas."

"I totally get it. My husband just wants to know the company we are spending thousands of dollars with is professional. You can tell so much about a company by the way they conduct business where the customers don't see."

"Oh, no doubt. I completely agree with you. I

pretty much hate stupid rules like that. Screw it. Come on back. No one is here anyway. I'll show you around."

"Sweet!" Jessica responded.

Miranda opened the small gate that separated the lobby from the work area and motioned for Jessica to come through. When Jessica joined her, she shut the gate and put a sign up, letting customers know she'd be back in five minutes.

"So, these are the offices. They're only used during the planning stages of construction or when it's slow out there in the field. This is a busy time of year for us and so I'm alone a lot of the time on most days. Although it gets lonely sometimes, I have plenty to do to keep me busy, and I don't have to put up with office bullshit."

"Yes!" Jessica said, laughing. "Office bullshit is the worst. I used to work for this prestigious…" Her voice trailed off as she remembered how her boss had hurt her—even destroyed her—a few years earlier.

Miranda, sensing that a difficult memory had hit Jessica, jumped in to pull her attention away from it. "I hear you. It's okay…don't even think about it. Let me show you the back."

Miranda opened a door that led from the office area back to the huge metal building behind it which was the shop area. Jessica quickly forgot about the painful memory as she saw the building. The ceiling was at least twenty feet high and the building was easily a hundred feet long. The right side of the building was all roll-up doors, one after another.

"The back half is where we store materials and supplies; anything left over from a job or anything we buy in bulk to get better pricing. The front half of the building is where we do some of our construction. We have a couple of skilled cabinet makers that work for us and we make many of our own cabinets, built-in entertainment centers and the like. When they don't have work here to do, they work out in the field."

Miranda took Jessica closer to one of the projects that was finished but waiting to be taken to a job site and installed. "This library wall was ordered for a custom library we are building for a local book collector. We basically added a thousand square feet to his house and it is all going to be books."

"This is amazing," Jessica said, looking around at the custom woodwork as well as the rows of saws, drill presses and other tools. "It's super clean as well."

"Well, the owners are a little OCD. They like a clean shop and aren't shy about letting someone know if they feel a work area is not up to snuff. They take a lot of pride in their business and their reputation."

"I know the feeling," Jessica acknowledged. "Reputation is everything. Once you lose that, you've lost it all." She paused, eying a wall of air tools, a compressor and an attached air hose.

"Yes, that is why we do so well here. Anyway, we should probably head back to the office. Let's chat a little more on what we can do for you." Miranda turned and took two steps toward the office door.

"Actually, let's talk about what *I* can do *to* you," Jessica said, picking up a three-foot piece of nearby two-by-two and slamming it into the back of Miranda's head.

chapter **five**

Jessica was hoping Miranda would go down and she wasn't disappointed. Dealing with a limp body was much easier than a fighting one.

Expecting she would hear if someone showed up, Jessica pulled on a pair of nitrile gloves she had in her pocket and got to work. She fired up the nearby compressor and attached the air hose to the nail gun, firing a test nail through the air. It flew across the shop and pinged off the far wall.

Smiling, Jessica grabbed approximately twelve two-by-fours off a nearby stack and started nailing them together to form a crude, box-style stand, which she left lying on the ground. Spotting a pallet filled with plywood sheets, Jessica slid one sheet off the stack and drug it over to the frame. Placing the plywood on top of the two-by-fours, Jessica fastened them together using the nail gun. When she was confident that the contraption would hold up, she dragged Miranda's body over to the wood and laid her flat on her back, her hands outstretched above her head. Jessica picked up Miranda's limp right hand and admired her fingernails. For being in the construction industry, Jessica could tell she didn't do any of the manual labor herself. The fingers—as well as the attached nails—were dainty and delicate. Jessica turned the small hand and placed the pale palm against the unforgiving wood surface. The nail gun did a fine job fastening the hand to the wood. Jessica added a few more nails just to make sure the flesh did not tear loose.

Satisfied with her handiwork, she secured the other hand and both feet to the plywood. When she was confident that Miranda wasn't going anywhere, Jessica hoisted the frame so that it was standing vertically. Once it was in the upright position, Jessica nailed a few more pieces of wood to the bottom frame to ensure it wouldn't tip over if Miranda woke up and started thrashing around.

With nothing to do but wait, Jessica picked up the piece of wood she had clubbed Miranda over the head with and took it to a planer machine. She had seen one in action before on television and decided to give it a try. After finding the power switch and firing up the piece of equipment, she pushed the board through the planer until one side of the wood had been stripped off, turning it into sawdust. She rotated the wood one turn and did the next side, then the last two sides. When she was done with it, she turned off the planer, dusted the sawdust from the area around it and returned the two-by-two, which was slightly thinner, to the pile it had come from. She certainly didn't want to leave any fingerprints behind.

Finally, when Jessica was satisfied that the only trail she left was Miranda-on-display, she sat down and waited, the air gun in her hand. She looked at her watch. Almost eleven o'clock. She wasn't sure if anyone would be by the shop around lunch, so she had to hurry. A groan brought her fully aware. Miranda was coming around.

"Heyyyy, sleepyhead," Jessica taunted.

Miranda's eyes flickered open and closed again as she regained full consciousness. When she finally became aware of her situation, panic washed over her face and she tried to pull her hands free, only to be overcome with excruciating pain. She screamed as the metacarpals ground against the shanks of the nails that held firm. One of the nails in her right hand had pierced the ulnar nerve, sending razor-sharp pain all the way up to her elbow. Blood oozed from her wounds, covering both hands in gloves of crimson.

"That looks like it hurts." Jessica winced in faux compassion. "Can I get you a Band-Aid?"

"My hands!" Miranda screamed. Tears poured down her cheeks. "Oh my God, my hands! You sick psycho piece-of-shit!"

Jessica clucked her tongue and frowned. "And your feet, darling. Don't forget your feet."

Miranda strained her neck trying to get a look at the damage. She only now became aware of the fire in her feet as nerves sparked and the initial shock of the wounds wore off. She saw the shiny nail heads jutting out of her flesh—at least eight, maybe more—and she started to hyperventilate. Her ragged breathing quickened, and she felt like she couldn't catch her breath.

"I don't think you'll be wearing sandals anymore," Jessica said, her voice calm and cool.

Miranda's head fell back against the wood frame that supported her body. She closed her eyes, focusing on trying to get control of her breathing. After a moment, she spoke, her voice timid, unintelligible.

"What was that?" Jessica asked, leaning forward. "I'm sorry, I didn't hear you, sweetie."

"Why?" Miranda finally managed. She opened

her eyes and turned her head slowly as she tried to study her limbs again. It hurt too much when she moved her head or body. She gave up quickly and fixed her frightened glare on Jessica.

"You should really be more careful who you let in the back."

"When I get out of here, I'm going to kill you. I'm going to destroy you and everything you ever loved," Miranda threatened through teeth clenched with pain.

"What makes you think you're getting out of this, you poor delusional soul?"

But, I was nice to you," Miranda whined. The constant throbbing in her appendages was ever present, making it hard to concentrate, to focus.

Jessica chuckled. "Do you really think I fell for that fake-ass bullshit? I know who you really are." Jessica raised the gun and fired a nail toward Miranda and hit her in the leg. Miranda screamed.

"Stop! Why are you doing this?"

"Cause I can."

Miranda squeezed her eyes shut and let out a groan, the pain overtaking her. She tasted the salt of her tears at the corners of her turned-down lips. "Listen, shithead, we don't keep money here," she said suddenly. “But I…you can take whatever I have in my purse.”

“I don’t want your damn money, you pathetic sow. I have my own; plenty of it.”

“Then what are you doing here?” Miranda asked, fear peeling away her anger and resolve. She couldn’t stop crying and her voice rose and fell as she tried to breathe in between. “Why are you doing *this*?”

Jessica seemed to be enjoying the other woman’s pain and fear and the raw emotion of it. She felt her nerves buzzing and her hands trembled slightly with anticipation. “There are things more important than money.”

“I still don’t understand what you’re talking about,” Miranda moaned.

“Didn’t you brag about how good your company’s reviews were?”

“Yes…why?…what does that have to do with this?”

“Reviews matter to me, too.”

“Whoever you are, this must be one big mistake.” She licked her lips and swallowed the thick mucus that had lined her mouth. Her eyes felt swollen and her head now throbbed in her temples. “Please, just leave. Just go. I won’t tell anyone who did this to me.”

“Oh, there is no mistake, Miranda Reads.” Jessica

fired another nail and this time, hit her other leg. She held the gun out in front of her and looked it over admiringly. "Wow, I'm pretty good at this if I do say so myself."

"Please stop…stop…no more," Miranda said in a defeated, quavering voice as the nail penetrated her flesh. The shock of the pain temporarily pulled her attention away from the fact that Jessica had just called her by her online reviewer name. Finally, when the agony receded a bit and she could concentrate, she responded. "Wait, what did you call me?"

"I'm pretty sure you heard me. Big, bad Miranda. Hiding behind a keyboard. Pretty tough when you're hidden behind a screen. You don't look so tough now."

Jessica smiled as the realization became evident in Miranda's eyes. Yes, she was definitely enjoying this, more so now as she watched Miranda trying to put the pieces of the puzzle together.

"Who…who are you?" Miranda pleaded, her eyes wide with tears, snot running from her nose and down her lips. "This can't be happening."

"*Just wait, it gets worse*!", Jessica said. "Ring a bell? It should."

Miranda's jaw dropped open, the realization of her actions taking hold. "No. No way." She sniffed, then closed her eyes and shook her head. She opened her eyes again and focused them on Jessica. She blinked back tears. "You can't be her. You don't look like the picture."

"It's an altered author photo. I value my privacy."

"You're…Karen Carter?" Her jaw dropped open and her lips trembled. "You mutilated me because of a stupid review? Your bitch ass crippled me because of this?"

Anger flashed through Jessica's mind and she shot another nail, pinning Miranda's left elbow to the wood. Miranda screamed louder this time, the pain shattering any resolve she had.

"My God, no more! Please!"

"You want me to stop?"

Miranda closed her eyes. "Yes, please stop."

"Apologize."

Miranda's eyes opened slowly, and she stared at Jessica—with rage and terror in her eyes—for several tense seconds and then, hoping to make it all go away, said, "I'm sorry."

"I don't believe it. Say it like you mean it."

"I'm sorry," Miranda sobbed. Her eyes opened wide and she inhaled deeply and declared loudly, "I'm sorry! I'm so, so sorry!"

Jessica clucked her tongue again. "You aren't sorry."

Miranda closed her eyes and sobbed. Her body trembled and her face scrunched up. She looked like she was having a particularly irritable bowel movement, which struck Jessica as funny.

"Aw, are you crying again?" she mocked. "You cry a lot."

"You put holes in me, you bitch!" Miranda screamed and broke down again, full on tears and snot.

Jessica sat back and crossed her left leg over her right and lay the nail gun on her lap. She watched the woman have her little breakdown. When it appeared Miranda was cried out, Jessica said, "Wanna try that apology again, cry baby?"

"I didn't mean it. Please forgive me," Miranda said softly, regaining a sliver of her composure, hoping that by being nice, she would convince Jessica to let her go. Miranda was in overwhelming pain. Everything hurt, from mutilated feet to the roots of her hair. "I didn't mean anything by it."

"You're just saying that to save your skin."

"It's true. I was just having a bad day and I took it out on you—your book. It was stupid."

Now Jessica rolled her eyes. "Please," she scoffed.

"I've read all your reviews, Miranda. You're a mean girl hiding behind a pretty girl image. But I see beneath your layer of fabricated perfection. You're just a vile, rank, piece of shit that delights in causing pain to others for sport."

"What the hell do you know, anyway?" Miranda snapped, losing her resolve again for a second. "You're just a poser bitch that can't take criticism." As quickly as the anger flared, she realized it would not help her under the circumstances and she started crying again.

Jessica ignored Miranda's comments—and her tears—and continued. "Consider that this isn't coming from me. It's coming from all the people that can't—or won't—defend themselves. It's coming from all the people that pour their hearts and their souls into creating something beautiful to entertain others."

Lifting the nail gun from her lap and leaning forward, Jessica frowned, her eyes growing serious. "You could have simply hated it and moved on. Instead, you had to try and destroy me with your words. Ironic, isn't it, that you hurt people with the tools of their trade, and I'm gonna destroy you with the tools of yours!"

Jessica fired another nail, this time hitting Miranda in the stomach.

"That one's gonna do some damage," she taunted,

as she watched Miranda start to shake, shock taking over her body.

"Please," Miranda whispered, knowing that her cause was hopeless, yet she tried to reason with the crazy woman. "I have a husband…a dog…and who will take care of my turtle? I'll never…leave a…bad review…again."

"That's the first right thing you've said all day," Jessica told her as she fired the nail gun at Miranda repeatedly, as fast as her finger could activate the trigger. Miniature spikes whizzed through the air, hitting Miranda's face, one catching her in the right eye, the others in the forehead, then the neck, before she fired multiple shots at Miranda's chest, hitting her lungs, one in her sternum and finally one piercing her heart. Jessica watched as the dying woman's breathing slowed and the rise and fall of her chest tapered. Within minutes, Miranda's head lulled to right—her one good eye remained open, peering at Jessica as though she were looking right into her soul—and then she was gone.

chapter six

As soon as Jessica got back to the condo, she chopped the nitrile gloves into small pieces and flushed them down the toilet. There was no other evidence to get rid of, thankfully. A check of the construction company premises after Miranda had expired revealed that the place didn't even have video cameras.

In the shower, she stayed until the water got cold, trying to wash at least a little portion of her guilt away. It nagged at her.

Typically, Jessica didn't feel guilty for any of her actions. Did that make her a sociopath? Sometimes she felt like she was. She wondered what the hell was wrong with her this time and thought maybe it was because Miranda had seemed so pleasant in real life.

She would have to think twice before getting to know someone she was going to kill in the future.

Mentally exhausted, Jessica poured a Jim Beam and Coke, promising herself she would stop at two. She ordered a lunch to be delivered—a sub sandwich, chips and a cookie. When it arrived, she ate it ravenously and lay down on the bed for a nap. Tomorrow, she would actually enjoy the rest of her vacation and she wouldn't be worrying about killing someone. Instead, she would enjoy the beach or the pool until she had to head back to Manhattan.

The rest of the week was uneventful, except for the moments of guilt creeping into her head occasionally while she was trying to enjoy the nice Tampa weather. Whenever it would get overwhelming, Jessica would pull back up Miranda's review and read it again, which usually did a great job at chasing the guilt from her mind.

The news channels had been all over the murder. While someone dying in Tampa wasn't uncommon, the method by which Miranda had died in itself was extreme and the press had a field day with it.

By the time the week ended and Jessica was packing to leave, she had won—her mind was free of any remorse and she was back to her usual self.

Miranda would no longer affect her career or her thoughts.

Back at home, Jessica settled back into her daily routine of writing. She spent time working between the series that Lana Brooks had started as well as her own series, publishing both under the Karen Carter pen name. She needed to maintain a steady pace of four books per year.

A few weeks after her return from Tampa, as she sat in her library one evening trying to write, Jessica's thoughts kept turning toward the hot men she had seen in Tampa. She chided herself for being anti-social and knew she was not far removed from a recluse. She liked men, but it had been a very long time since she had been in a man's presence, let alone naked between the sheets with one. She had never been married, probably because she was difficult to live with and none of her relationships had even become serious.

Knowing she didn't have the time or energy for a relationship anyway, Jessica decided to do what she did best; find a man she could use once or twice, before she shut him out. It wouldn't matter, because the guy would probably only want to "hit it and quit it" anyway.

Jessica shut her laptop, her amatory thoughts taking over her mind. She had heard about an app called Tinder and deciding she would see what it was all about, she downloaded it. Soon, she was swiping left for every man's picture that came up. None of them resonated with her and she was one that had to feel the right vibe.

After dozens of swipes, she stopped. The eyes looking back at her looked kind. She certainly could use kind. Ethan Duke was his name. As she held her finger over the picture, she hesitated. If she swiped left again, she would never know if she would have had a good time with this guy for one or two nights. If she swiped right, she would be exposing herself to possible pain and anguish.

Jessica thought back to that night in the office with her boss. The last night she ever worked for him. The last time she felt safe with a man. Her former boss had taken way more from her than her dignity. He had taken away everything she was and turned her into a person she no longer recognized. She wondered what good it would do to go on a date with his man

—if he also swiped right. Could her instincts be wrong, resulting in her being on the brutal end of another assault?

A shudder went up Jessica's spine as she decided to abandon her plan of getting a quickie. She would have to be satisfied with the adjustable handheld showerhead in her bathroom. As she touched the screen to swipe the app up and close it, her finger slipped and the picture swiped right. Realizing her error, she quickly exited the app. Even if the guy swiped right on her too, she would never know since she would not be going back to look.

Jessica poured herself a glass of wine and went back into her library, bringing up her latest manuscript. She tried to get into the story and her mind tore her focus away from the words on the screen. As she wrestled with her concentration, she tried to be productive, yet her mind would not play ball.

Frustrated, she took out her phone, paused and opened up the Tinder app again, even though she had promised herself that she wouldn't. Shocked, she noticed that Ethan was a match. He had swiped right, also. There was a message waiting from him.

Hi, beautiful. I'm so happy to see we are a match. Drinks tonight?

Jessica felt herself blushing. It had been a long time since she felt the attention of a man. She closed the app again as her heart started pounding rapidly in her chest cavity. *What the hell am I doing?*

Jessica fought against her will, trying not to open the app again, but parts of her really wanted this. She tried not to listen to those parts of her, but they were very convincing. Jessica opened Tinder once again and replied.

Pocket Bar – Hell's Kitchen? 10 pm?

Jessica waited a few minutes and received no response. Knowing that she would be getting nothing written no matter what, she shut off the lights in the library and went to her closet, looking for something to wear. She settled on a short red dress that clung to her curves.

Jessica looked at the phone again. There was a message from Ethan.

Looking forward to it. I'll see you then. I'll be wearing a black button-down shirt. I look just like my picture. Can't miss me. Text me when you get there and I'll do the same.

Jessica saw the number pop up on the screen and she added it to the contacts in her phone.

I'll be the one in the red dress. I guarantee you won't miss me!

After a quick shower, Jessica slipped on her dress and did her hair. Checking the time on her phone, she put on her makeup and made sure she looked irresistible. When she was satisfied, she ordered an Uber, noting it was five minutes out. Slipping a knife out of the drawer in the kitchen and sliding it into her purse—just in case—she made her way to the lobby. When she saw the car pull up, she took a deep breath and stepped out to the curb. She was out of her comfort zone and would be until she got to know Ethan a little. Hopefully it wouldn't be awkward.

chapter seven

Jessica's eyes popped open and she glanced at the clock on the side table. It was a quarter after six in the morning. Sliding out from under the covers, she looked around the room for her clothes. Her panties were on her side of the bed, but she found her bra by the foot of the king-sized footboard. Her dress was in the hallway and her shoes in the living room. It had been a night.

Slinking through the apartment quietly, she got dressed as she tried not to wake Ethan up. She had a great time with him and he turned out to be a really nice guy, but she didn't want it to get weird. She would leave before he knew she was gone, even though she was tempted to wake him up and go for another round.

She thought back to the bar. She indeed recognized him immediately and he her. He definitely knew how to make her feel comfortable instantly by giving her a long hug when they approached each other. That hug—as delicious as it had been—set the tone for the remainder of the night.

A few drinks each and an Uber ride later and Jessica had found herself in his bed. She certainly hadn't put up a fight…she had wanted it probably more than he did.

With shoes in hand, Jessica found her purse on the couch and went back to the bedroom door to peak in on him. The sheets were halfway pulled off and his tight buns were facing her as he lay half on his side and half on his stomach. His sandy hair was a little shaggy, but well maintained. He was in wonderful shape, which she noticed gave him great stamina. Ethan had been a welcome distraction, but it was time to go.

As Jessica turned away from the doorway to slip out and catch a ride home, Ethan's voice trailed after her.

"Leaving without breakfast?"

Jessica turned back toward the room. "That was the plan."

"Can the plan be changed?"

"I can be convinced."

"What will it take to convince you?"

Jessica dropped her purse and shoes and slipped her dress off, letting it slide to the floor. "Dessert before breakfast."

Ethan sat up. "Twist my arm, why don't you?" he said, smiling.

Jessica slipped back over to the bed and climbed in. "Better hold on," she told him as she pushed him back onto the mattress.

When Jessica got back to her apartment that afternoon, she was exhausted. They had gone for a second round and then Ethan took her out for a nice breakfast at a nearby café. From there, she had grabbed a ride straight home, but not before he had made her agree to a second date.

As the shower washed the night of sweat and debauchery from her skin, she wondered what she had gotten herself into. She really liked the guy and he had been great company—both in and out of the bedroom—but she wasn't mentally able to get into a relationship, so why did she agree to see him again? Besides, if he was on Tinder, he was probably bedding any hot chick that swiped right. Jessica certainly hadn't put up a struggle.

Clean and feeling human again, Jessica slipped into her bed, the silk sheets caressing her smooth skin as she covered herself. A nap was in order. It would be dark before she woke.

That evening, Jessica awoke refreshed, surprised to find herself in a chipper mood. She attributed it to the sex.

As she checked her messages, she noticed a text from Ethan.

Dinner?

She responded.

Not tonight. I need to recover. LOL

Jessica hesitated, then typed *Tomorrow?*

She waited a minute and then two, but there was no response. Had she upset him? Her phone finally chimed.

8:00? I'll pick you up.

Jessica paused, then throwing out all abandon, she texted him the address. If worse came to worse and he started acting crazy, building security would keep him out.

Finished with her messages, Jessica went to her library, took care of a couple of things for her publisher and then opened the manuscript she had abandoned the night before. The words flowed from her fingertips and two hours later, she looked to find she had typed over four thousand words. She was back. She had simply needed to clear her mind.

Over the next few weeks, Jessica finished the book she had been working on and found time to see Ethan a few times a week. She'd no idea how he kept up with her, but he certainly kept her satisfied—to the point that her muscles were always sore.

What she had anticipated being a one or two-time bootie call had evolved. They were actually dating which not only shocked the hell out of Jessica, but according to Ethan, it shocked him as well. He hadn't been looking for a relationship either. Relationships sometimes blossomed out of the most carnal situations and this was one of those times.

It was actually after one of their dates—Ethan had taken her on a surprise date to the New York Catacombs by Candlelight, which was a tour of the catacombs of the historical Basilica of St. Patrick's Old Cathedral—that her world was rocked one more time.

With life keeping her busy and there being no time to concentrate on negative things, Jessica hadn't checked her book reviews in weeks. That night, she spent an hour reading reviews on various sites, rolling her eyes at some of the lackluster ones while smiling at the good ones. It was when she went to Amazon that she saw the one-star review.

The overwhelming feeling that Jessica hadn't felt in weeks slipped back into her mind and took over all her thoughts. Anger seethed from her pores as she tried to control herself.

Trembling, Jessica went to the kitchen and poured a short glass of Maker's Mark, knowing that wine was not going to cut it. As she took big gulps, she read the review once again, knowing she would need to do something about it.

Who the F**K is Karen Carter?

Karen Carter, if that is her real name, is nothing

but a poser. It's easy to see she isn't the one that wrote the previous books. Perhaps she hired several ghost-writers to make up for her lack of imagination and talent, but any friggin idiot can see that many of these books were written by different authors. She's nothing but a hack sitting behind a computer screen faking being a bestselling author. I hope she gets exposed for what she really is.

As Jessica read the review for the fourth time, she began to wonder if the reviewer knew her deep, dark secrets, but how could they? There was no one that knew her transgressions besides her.

Jessica felt her body involuntarily shudder as she considered the repercussions of being found out. She could not have people talking and getting suspicious over who she really was. That would only lead to questions about Lana Brooks. She was living in Lana's apartment pretending to be her. She couldn't afford any scrutiny.

Calming herself down, Jessica logged into the Amazon employee portal to get the reviewer's information. As she dug through the records, a thought hit her and she started looking for a function to remove the review. She had never before done so and apparently, neither had Lana, as all of the shitty reviews directed at her and her books still existed.

After an hour of digging, Jessica found herself in an application that would let her remove the review. She paused with her finger ready to click the mouse, hoping that making changes wouldn't come back at her as she knew her IP address would most likely show up in the system.

"Screw it!" Jessica clicked the button. The review disappeared. It had been so easy. Her thoughts went back to the other reviews she would love to see gone. Especially Miranda's. Jessica pulled up Miranda's review, her finger hovering over the delete button. Finally, she clicked out of the application, not wanting to take a chance by deleting more than just the one review.

Breathing a sigh of relief, Jessica went back to the customer information she had looked at earlier and drilled down to the contact information of the reviewer. As she read the address she blinked, reading it again to make sure she wasn't imagining things. The reviewer was from the City of Orange in California. Did Jessica know this person? While Jessica believed in some coincidences, this was too much. Clasping her elbows, she took shallow breaths and tried to think. How could this have happened? She had been so careful.

When she regained her composure, Jessica jotted

down notes about the person, whose name was Amanda Barrett. The name didn't ring a bell. As Jessica wrote down the address, she looked it up on Google maps and noticed the address was across town from her old house. How could this person know who she was or what she'd done? The more information she learned, the more confused she became.

After learning everything she could, she booked a flight to California. She would leave in two days. She had to regulate the problem. Amanda Barrett wouldn't know what hit her.

chapter eight

"You okay?" Ethan asked.

Jessica looked up from her plate and forced a smile. "Sorry, I was just thinking about work. I have to go on a business trip the day after tomorrow."

She hadn't told Ethan she was a writer. Instead, she told him she was in publishing and he hadn't asked too many questions about it.

Knowing she wouldn't see him for a week or so, Jessica had asked him if he wanted to grab dinner.

"Where you heading?"

"California."

"What's going on there?"

"I have to meet with a client."

"Lucky you. I've always enjoyed visiting California."

"Yeah, me too," she said, not volunteering she used to live there.

"How long will you be gone?"

"A few days to a week, tops."

"What am I gonna do with you out of town?"

"Whoever you want," she smirked.

"Funny! I'm actually not seeing anyone else…you ruined it for me."

"I don't know whether to be flattered or…" Her voice dropped off, a sly smile lacing her lips.

"Oh, be flattered. It's a compliment, trust me."

"I'll take your word for it," she laughed.

They finished their dinner and Ethan invited Jessica back to his apartment for the night.

"I'd love to," Jessica said, letting out a heavy sigh, "but I have too much on my mind. How about when I get back?"

"It's a date," he acknowledged. "Just text me when you get back and we can set something up."

"Deal."

After dinner, they walked outside together and they hailed Jessica a cab. Ethan lived a couple of blocks away from the restaurant and he would walk home. Before she got in the cab, Ethan gave her a big hug and a deep kiss. Confused as to the emotions she was feeling, she climbed into the cab and shut the door, switching her thoughts to her upcoming trip.

As the plane touched down at John Wayne airport, Jessica closed her eyes and took a calming breath. Considering why she had come back to California, she had a little trepidation. She waited until everyone else got off the plane and then grabbed her carry-on and went to the baggage area.

When she had retrieved her one suitcase, she made her way to the car rental area and picked up her car, entering Amanda's address into the GPS on her phone before exiting the garage. She took a drive by Amanda's house before heading to her hotel, just to get her bearings on where it was located. When she arrived and checked in, she unpacked her things and went down to the hotel bar. There was no way she was going to do anything until at least the next day and as soon as this little problem was dealt with, she would be on the next plane home.

After her second drink, she ordered a cheeseburger and fries and polished everything off with a third drink. She was surprised that no one tried to hit on her, but maybe it was because she was greedily stuffing her mouth with food.

Back in her room, Jessica turned on HBO and watched the movie that was playing as she tried to mentally prepare for what was to come. In the morning, she would scope out the situation.

When the alarm on her phone went off, Jessica woke with a start, unsure of where she was for a moment. When she finally remembered, she felt a heavy weight in her stomach as she mentally prepared for the day.

After a quick shower and getting dressed, she got in the rental car and drove off, skipping breakfast in the process. Her stomach wasn't in any shape to be adding food at the current moment.

She drove the few miles to Amanda's house. The street was quiet and Jessica remembered the house from the day before as it was a drab, white, single-story in the middle of the block. There was one car in the driveway. From what she uncovered during her research, she was under the impression that Amanda

Barrett was single. She hoped that was the case as it would make things easier.

Jessica looked at her watch—7:30 am. She waited and watched as neighboring cars left their driveways. Soon it was 8:00 am and there was still no movement. The minutes ticked by and Jessica was starting to lose her mind from boredom when at 8:37 am, she saw the front door open and a figure emerged.

Jessica didn't know what she was expecting, but it wasn't this. Amanda Barrett, if that was her, was about 4'8" and half as wide. She barely cleared the door without having to turn sideways. She wore a faded pair of jeans and a plaid blouse. Her dark hair touched her shoulders and framed her pale face, her pink, plastic hairclip being the most prominent feature. Otherwise, she was vapidly plain.

Amanda peered up and down the street before climbing into her car, a tan Ford Taurus as uninspiring as she was. When she backed out and started down the street, Jessica pulled out and followed from a distance. Cautiously, she weaved in and out of traffic and ten minutes later, followed Amanda into an Albertson's parking lot.

Expecting Amanda to go on a shopping trip, Jessica was shocked when she pulled a green apron from the back seat of the car and put it on. Apparently, Amanda worked there.

Giving Amanda a fifteen-minute head start, Jessica entered the store from the other entrance and plucked a hand basket from the stand by the door. Inside, she grabbed a couple of items she needed and a bottle of water, watching for Amanda as she made her way around the store. When she walked around the end by the bakery, she noticed Amanda behind the deli counter slicing cheese for a customer.

Before Amanda could turn around, Jessica slipped around the corner and to the front of the store. Using the self-checkout registers, Jessica paid cash and exited the building.

Back in her car, Jessica left the parking lot and headed back to Amanda's house. She knew she had some time since Amanda had just clocked in at work.

When Jessica reached Amanda's street, she drove past the house and pulled into the next block, finding a parking space against the curb. The walk back to Amanda's house was a quick one and the day was mild and sunny. As she neared the house, she watched the neighbors' houses carefully, anticipating movement from any of them. A dog barked from farther down the block, but Jessica sensed no movement.

At Amanda's front door, Jessica knocked and

waited for a response. She hadn't quite prepared what she'd say if someone answered, but in her mind, she felt like maybe she'd pretend it was a religious call. A second knock that went unanswered calmed her nerves and after one last cursory look around, Jessica slipped behind a hedge and around the side of the house. Her left arm scraped against the beige stucco and she pulled it back, rubbing the abrasion in irritation, before she ducked through a side gate and around the back of the house.

As she approached the back door, her heart jumped as she heard a dog bark, this time close by. She stopped in her tracks and listened. No more barking. As she stepped toward the door, she heard the bark again and this time she pinpointed it as being in the neighbor's yard. Unfortunately, it had sensed her, but the cement block wall afforded privacy allowing her to move around without being seen.

Jessica slipped on a pair of nitrile gloves before trying the door handle, but it was locked. She made her way around the other side and saw a low window that had an open view of the interior of the house. Jessica peered in and noticed a spa tub on the other side of the window. The bathroom was beautifully decorated with candles, knickknacks and luxurious towels. Whoever this Amanda person was, she sure knew how to beautify her home. Hoping she could get in through that window, Jessica pulled the screen off and pressed up on the glass. It slid up vertically and she threw one leg over the sill and climbed inside.

As she exited the bathroom, she noticed she was in the master bedroom. Digging through drawers and the closet, Jessica didn't notice any men's clothing nor did it look like there were toiletries for two in the bathroom. Inspections of the other rooms in the house verified Jessica's suspicions. The second bathroom had no personal effects in it and one of the other two bedrooms had a bed and dresser, but no clothes in it or the closet. The last bedroom had a small desk and a chair and appeared to be used as an office. Things were looking up.

On her second trip through the small home, Jessica closely studied each room and its contents. She looked in every drawer to see if there were weapons stashed about, but the main tools of destruction and death were in the kitchen. There was no garage.

Deciding she would enter the house the next morning while Amanda was sleeping, she took one last look around the home, making sure she would remember the layout for her early morning visit. As she opened the back door and twisted the lock, she stepped out and as she was about to pull the door shut behind her, it hit her. She would not surprise Amanda Barrett in the morning while she was sleeping. She would surprise her tonight when Amanda arrived home from work.

Back inside, Jessica went into the kitchen and made herself a sandwich. She would be settling in for the long haul.

chapter nine

The sun slipped over the house and to the west as the day slowly ate away at Jessica's nerves. Not knowing if Amanda was working four hours, eight or anything in between, she was very careful with her actions and was on guard throughout the day.

The first two hours, she planned her attack. She knew exactly where she would hide. She knew where she would attack and she had her instrument of destruction chosen and beside her. Instead of taking one of the gleaming knives out of the butcher block—a missing knife would surely be noticed—she dug around in the utensil drawers and ended up finding an ice pick. It would be easy to swing and easy to puncture. She just had to make sure it hit its mark.

Bored beyond belief, Jessica wished she had her

phone with her, but she left it in the hotel just in case as she didn't want it pinging on cell phone towers in the area should she ever become a suspect.

She didn't dare turn on the TV as she might get distracted and not hear her intended victim come in. She couldn't afford to get careless. She had to concentrate.

In the living room, she found a sizable bookshelf that she hadn't paid much attention to earlier. She perused the titles and was surprised to find a complete representation of every Karen Carter book that existed, amongst other authors. Even the book that Jessica had written in the new series, as well as the ones she had finished after she killed Lana, were on the shelf. It appeared Amanda Barrett was a super-fan. Had she really noticed a difference in the writing? Even Lana's agent and Random House hadn't made any mention of a change in style—how could this troll that worked in the deli at the local Albertsons have noticed?

Jessica ran her fingers down the spine of some of the paperbacks. They were well-read, indicating they had either been purchased used, or Amanda had read them multiple times each. *Could she really know my secret?*

As four hours passed, then five, six and seven,

Jessica started preparing herself—she would need to get into her hiding spot soon, which she had earlier picked out as the closet in the spare bedroom. There would be no reason for Amanda to go into that room —and especially the closet—as it was empty and appeared to be unused.

If Amanda were to come straight home after work, and she worked an eight-hour shift, she would be home within an hour and a half.

Jessica's plan was fairly straight-forward. She couldn't risk the neighbor's dog barking or Amanda hearing a noise while she tried to get back into the house, so she had decided to stay, hide and wait for Amanda to go to sleep. She would attack her while she slumbered, which meant she might be waiting in the closet for a very long time.

In the kitchen, Jessica looked at the clock on the microwave. It was 5:15 pm and she felt deep down inside that Amanda would be home fairly soon. Looking around to make sure that nothing was out of place, she made her way to the spare bedroom, entered the closet and sat on the floor as she slid the door shut behind her. The darkness enveloped her and she could make out nothing in the small space.

Trying to get comfortable, Jessica stretched out the full length of the closet, her fingers intertwined behind her head, her eyes closed and her ears listening for the slightest sound.

Minutes went by and then what seemed like half an hour passed with no action. Jessica went back through her guestimated timeframes in her mind and wondered if Amanda had gone out after work or went to run an errand. From what Jessica had seen of Amanda's house, it didn't look like Amanda had much of a life besides books. Then it hit Jessica. She hadn't accounted for a lunch hour. Her timeframes could be off by thirty to sixty minutes.

Rather than get back out of her hiding spot and get caught off guard, she continued to wait in the dark, her heartbeat the only sound. Adrenaline coursed through her body keeping her on high alert, so there was no danger in her drifting off to sleep.

After approximately another hour, Jessica thought she heard a door opening. Her senses perked up and she listened carefully. Sounds of someone in the other room: a door being shut followed by the clank of keys being dropped on the counter. Amanda Barrett was home.

Jessica continued to listen, trying to match actions in her mind to the sounds she heard, which were muffled due to the closed closet doors. A toilet flushing. A refrigerator door opening and closing.

Items being set down on the counter in the kitchen. The possible preparation of a meal.

Jessica stayed on point the entire time, the icepick steadied at her right side in case she needed to strike quickly. Luckily, should she be discovered, she would have the element of surprise.

Approximately twenty minutes later, she heard more rattling in the kitchen and then she heard a TV come on. From the distant sound of it, she assumed it was the living room television. Jessica certainly hadn't expected Amanda to go to bed this early, but she was getting impatient and wanted to get the deed out of the way. As she toyed with the idea of sneaking into the living room and completing what she was there for, she heard the TV get louder. It sounded like the news was on.

Jessica mentally walked back through the placement of the living room furniture in her mind. If she slipped into the hall, she would be able to peer down it and see part of the living room at the opposite end. While she could most likely see the television screen, the couch and Lay-Z-Boy chair were up against the wall off to the right and Amanda would be facing away from the hall. If Jessica were quiet, she could easily sneak up on Amanda, punch her in the neck or heart with the icepick, watch her bleed out and be on her way. She decided to wait a little while longer to make sure Amanda was settled in and then she would strike.

Half an hour more passed and Jessica heard the news show end and another show start. Five minutes later, she slid the closet door open a few inches and listened. The only sounds were from the television. The bedroom remained dark except for the minimal light that made its way to the space from the living room. While she had been in the closet, the sun had disappeared and no light filtered through the windows.

Jessica slid the door all the way open, thankful that it moved smoothly and silently on its tracks. She crawled out from her hiding spot, slid the door shut and crawled behind the side of the bed where she couldn't be seen if someone walked by from the hallway and looked in. From her new hiding spot, she listened more intently for any sounds other than the TV. She heard nothing.

Peering over the bed, Jessica looked out at the doorway across the hall which was the master bedroom. The door was open and the room was dark. Confident that the intended victim was watching TV and oblivious to the impending doom she faced, Jessica stood up and readied the icepick at her side.

Thankful that the room and hallway were carpeted, she stepped lightly and made sure she wasn't clumsy enough to trip over the corner of the bed.

From the hall, Jessica saw the television flicker as the show entertained the living room's only occupant. Jessica felt sorry for Amanda for a moment, but as she did, she mentally chastised herself and pulled the memory of the latest review back into her head. She would not feel remorse for this murder. The troll had it coming.

chapter **ten**

Jessica stayed close to the wall as she crept her way out to the living room. She kept her breath slow and deliberate. The remainder of the house was quiet and dark, making her mission easier. Maybe if she was lucky, Amanda would have fallen asleep in her favorite chair.

As Jessica approached the end of the hall, she stopped short of the room, paused and peered around the corner. She was able to see the full length of the couch. It wasn't occupied. That left the chair, which she could only see the back of, but knowing Amanda's height, she could easily be sitting there. There was nowhere else she could be.

Urging herself to act, Jessica charged toward the chair, half running and half diving at it, bringing the steel from the pick down hard, hoping to drive it into Amanda's neck. She caught herself and fully brought her body upright when she realized the chair was empty. It was then she heard the voice as someone stepped from the shadows of the hallway.

"You didn't really think I would be *that* stupid, did you?" Amanda asked.

Although caught off guard, Jessica was still quick to recover from the shock of seeing Amanda there. "Actually, I was pretty certain of it."

"Looks like you need to do your homework better."

Jessica snickered. "No matter. Living room, hallway, even your bedroom. The outcome will still be the same."

Amanda stepped out of the shadows and Jessica instantly became aware of the pistol at her side.

"Damn straight," Amanda sneered. "Stupid bitch brought an icepick to a gunfight."

Jessica's eyes went wide and she involuntarily held her hands out in front of her. "No need to get crazy. I'm sure we can talk this out."

"Why on earth would I need to talk about this?" Amanda challenged. "You broke into my house. I can shoot you dead."

"You'd go to jail."

"Silly girl. You're from California. You should know that as long as I feel my life is in danger, I have that right...and I'll get off Scott-free. You have an ice pick in your hand. What else do I need?"

"How did you know I was here?"

"I figured you might show up at some point in time. I really wasn't expecting you before..." her voice trailed off. Finally, she continued. "I probably wouldn't have known, but I had a sandwich for dinner tonight. Funny thing is, the top of the bread bag was folded under, without the twist-tie. I live alone, so things are typically the way I leave them. That's when I really knew."

Jessica stood, frozen in her tracks, not sure of what to do about this sudden turn of events. Killing Lana Brooks had been so much easier. She kept the element of surprise and there was no gun involved. In this case, she had screwed herself. She tried to speak, but the words would no longer fall from her lips. How could this troll be expecting her? Did Amanda know who she was? It didn't make sense.

"How was your plane ride, Jessica?"

Jessica's mouth fell open. "How do you know who I am?"

"Who else would be in my house right now?"

"You don't know anything," Jessica scoffed.

"Well it's pretty easy to tell you aren't really Karen Carter."

"No one is Karen Carter."

"Good point, but I noticed the difference in prose immediately."

"Impossible," Jessica spat.

"Doesn't matter what you think. I know who you are and why you're here. In fact, I left that review to make you nervous. I thought it would take you a little longer before you showed up though."

"Do we know each other?" Jessica asked, her mind racing, searching for answers.

"Surprisingly, no," Amanda confirmed. "And I've lived here my whole life."

"Well I'm not from here. I'm from New York."

"Once again, you act like I'm stupid. You only moved to Manhattan after you took over Lana Brook's life. Before that, you lived right here in Orange. And speaking of Lana Brooks, what happened to her? Did you kill her? I'm sure the cops would be interested in that story."

Jessica was dumfounded, brutally aware that she was on the losing end of the equation. She felt her stomach twist up in knots. Finally, she dropped her air of superiority—she certainly was at a disadvantage—approaching Amanda from a more subdued tone.

"You obviously have me dead to rights. I've met my match. What is it you want from me? Money? Just name your price." Jessica winced at the irony considering Miranda had offered money too, as a barter for living.

"I don't want your damn money," Amanda snarled. "You break into my house to kill me and you think that throwing money at the situation will appease me? How do I know you won't come back?"

"With what I can pay you, you can disappear to places I could never find you."

"Wake up and smell the desperation, Jessica. I'm not falling for your crap. You have to be stopped and I'm the only one who knows everything."

"How?" Jessica asked. "I have to know how *you* know who I am—what I came here for."

"Did you see my bookcase?"

"I did."

"I'm a huge Karen Carter fan. I knew something was off the moment I saw one of your books. At first, I thought it was my imagination, but the more I studied your new books and compared them to the old ones, I could tell someone else was writing them. I just couldn't figure out why, and there was no information on the web."

"That's cause no one knows. Not even my publisher."

"That makes sense."

"Still, how do you know who I am? How did you figure it out?"

"Stupid luck."

Jessica leaned against the wall, unsure of what was coming next, but exhausted to the core. "How so?" she asked.

"My computer died."

"And?"

"I had to get another one."

Jessica sighed and rolled her eyes. "Are you really going to make me pull this out of you one sentence at a time?"

Amanda sneered, making it evident she was enjoying the exchange. "I bought a used one from the Salvation Army. I have to say I was surprised when it worked like a champ. Even more surprised when I found the previous owner hadn't erased the drive."

Jessica blinked rapidly as she tried to process this new information. Laptop. Salvation Army. What had she done with her old laptop? Certainly, she had packed it in the boxes with the rest of her personal effects, hadn't she? It had to be in the boxes that were still sitting in the spare bedroom in her apartment.

She wouldn't have just given that computer away, even though she had started using Lana's MacBook. Was Amanda inferring she had Jessica's old one?

"What was on those drives?" Jessica whispered.

"I think you know."

"I need to hear it."

"Pretty interesting how the first book in the new Karen Carter series is on my new laptop in manuscript form, but the author's name is Jessica Nichols. Anyone you know?"

Jessica wavered on her feet, almost losing her balance. She felt light-headed, still trying to connect the dots. Her next question came out in a whisper. "What else?"

"Pretty interesting program on that laptop. When I click it, I see activity from someone else's computer. Lana Brooks' computer. Only it isn't Lana Brooks using it anymore, is it?"

Her worst fears realized, Jessica slid down the wall and slumped on the floor. Amanda Barrett had beat her at her own game. She had everything. She could single-handedly destroy her. It was over. She was defeated.

"Get up!" Amanda shouted, raising the pistol in Jessica's direction. "I need you on the couch now while I figure out what to do next."

"Are you going to shoot me?" Jessica asked weakly.

"I'd planned on it, but now I'm rethinking things. Unless you try something. Then I won't hesitate to shoot you in your fool head."

"Why?" Jessica asked, raising her hand questioningly. "Why all this? Why didn't you just call the police as soon as you knew?"

"Simple. I hate you and everything you are. You took away my only companion—my Karen Carter books. Nothing is the same now. I've had fantasies of making you pay. Now that I'm in the situation, I'm not sure I have the stomach for it. When it comes down to it, I'm not you. I wouldn't be able to live with myself. The police will have to sort it all out. Now get your ass on the couch, so I can keep you in sight while I get to the phone."

"Amanda, listen to me," Jessica pleaded with newfound courage, hoping one last time to buy her silence. "I have millions. I'll give you half. You'll never want for anything again. You'll never be lonely again."

Amanda paused, pushing her hair out of her face with her left hand. "Well…"

"Please Amanda. This will be our secret."

"I…how can I…trust you?"

"You have the gun. You have all the power. You

know everything. I can transfer the money to you and you can be gone. No more shitty deli department job. No more lonely nights eating sandwiches for dinner. Think about it."

Amanda took a deep breath and ran her fingers through her hair. "No…I don't…I don't know. Get up. On the couch. I…I can't…I need to think. I'm serious right now. MOVE!" The pistol shook in her hand as she yelled.

Jessica hesitated, then slowly pulled herself to her knees.

"Nice and slow!" Amanda growled. "I don't want to shoot you. I don't!"

"Easy," Jessica coaxed. "I'm gonna stand up slowly. Please don't shoot me."

"Just take it easy."

Jessica pulled one foot under herself and lifted her body off the floor and then pushed up with her hands. Amanda placed both hands on the grip of the pistol and Jessica noticed her hands shaking more, a fraction of a second before Jessica spun around, launched the pick at Amanda's face and ducked into a roll toward her. Jessica didn't know if the thin, metal shank did any damage, if it bounced off her face handle first or if it missed its mark completely, but she was hoping that Amanda would be stunned long enough for her to get the upper hand.

As Jessica rolled toward Amanda's legs, she not only made herself a moving target, but she hoped to take control of the situation. Amanda went down like a sack of potatoes and landed on her back, the thud quite impressive even though the carpet somewhat cushioned the blow. Jessica pounced on Amanda's gun hand and pulled the pistol from her grip. Amanda did not fight back. The fall must have knocked the air out of her.

Scrambling to her feet, Jessica aimed the pistol at Amanda and flipped the hallway light switch. Jessica froze, her eyes wide in shock. The ice pick had made its mark after all. Jessica felt her stomach heave as the wooden handle and only an inch of the steel protruded from Amanda's right eye. Jessica winced as she stared at the pick and then as she remembered the nail that had punctured Miranda's eye back in Florida.

Shit. Is she dead? she thought. Glancing at Amanda's chest, she noticed it rising and falling. Not dead after all. Unconscious maybe or possibly just in shock. Jessica ran past her into the master bedroom and pulled the garbage liner out of the bathroom trashcan, dumping the trash on the carpet as she ran back toward the hallway. Reconsidering, she ran back into the bedroom and slipped the gun between the mattress and the box spring. There would be no gunfire happening if she had anything to do with it. She didn't need that kind of attention.

Back out in the hall, Amanda was getting up off the floor. Jessica stopped and stood back, watching Amanda turn around facing her, the icepick protruding, bouncing around as she moved. The scene was straight out of a movie.

"I...I've changed...my mind," Amanda whispered, her face as white as a sheet. "I'm going to kill you after all."

Jessica dropped the trash liner, her hopes of finishing the job with a simple suffocation dashed. She dove at Amanda and they both went down again, fists flying. Amanda was able to roll as they landed and she came out on top of Jessica, her hands around Jessica's throat. Dazed by what had just happened, as well as struggling to suck the sweet, sweet oxygen into her lungs, she clawed at Amanda's hands to get her off, but Amanda had a death grip that Jessica was unable to thwart.

As Jessica's brain fogged up, she thought about how ridiculous the situation was. She had underestimated Amanda Barrett and now she was being strangled by her—strangled by a woman that had a damned ice pick protruding from her frigging eye. It didn't get more ironic than that.

In a last-ditch effort, Jessica tore at the flesh of Amanda's fingers, but her grip held fast, the grasp unrelenting and unyielding. Jessica's field of vision blackened at the edges, then the sensation started to warp inward.

"NO ONE stabs me in the eye with an ice pick and lives to tell about it!" Amanda screamed, spittle hitting Jessica in the face. "DIE, BITCH!"

A spark went off in Jessica's dying brain. *Icepick!*

With the last strength she had, Jessica released Amanda's hands, reached up, grabbed the handle of the icepick and pulled with all of her remaining strength, the instrument of destruction dislodging from the eyeball as Amanda released Jessica's throat, a scream ripping through the house. The sudden rush of oxygen gave Jessica the final push she needed and she slammed the icepick as hard as she could into Amanda's right ear. The thin sliver of steel found its mark and sank as deep as the handle would allow. The screaming immediately stopped. Jessica looked up at Amanda's face, the one good eye returning a glossed over stare. When Jessica twisted from underneath her,

Amanda fell over, her head smashing against the wall. She remained still.

Coughing and hacking, her windpipe on fire, Jessica scrambled to her feet and tried to regain her focus. She knew she needed to get out of there quickly as the scream was sure to have alerted the neighbors. Kneeling, Jessica checked Amanda's pulse. It was faint, but she could still feel it. She paused and continued to monitor it, noticing that it was fading quickly. When she could no longer feel the pulse, and Amanda's chest no longer rose and fell, Jessica stood back up and tried to get her bearings. She knew she had not brought anything into the house beside what she was wearing, so she simply needed to get the hell out of there.

Unlocking the front door, Jessica poked her head outside and looked around. There did not appear to be anyone paying attention, but she wasn't taking any chances. She locked the doorknob and pulled the door shut behind her, heading down the sidewalk toward where her car was parked.

A hundred feet down the sidewalk and it hit her. Turning back, she ran to the front door and tried to open it, but it was locked tight. A distant siren sliced through the air. Jessica stepped back and fired a hard kick at the door and it splintered in its frame, the door handle slamming against the inner wall.

Inside, Jessica ran back to the bedroom that Amanda had used as an office. On the desk was a laptop. Jessica's old laptop. There was no way she could leave it behind again. It would be her undoing.

With laptop in hand, she ran into the master bedroom and opened the closet, pulling out a hoodie and slipping into it, yanking the hood tight over her face.

Back outside the front of the house, Jessica ducked her head, crossed the street and ran as fast as she could to the next block where her car was parked, the volume of the sirens increasing every second. Jessica started the car, flipped a U-turn and started zigzagging through cross streets until she was out of the area. Finally, she hopped on one of the main streets and worked her way back to the hotel, where she used her keycard to slip in a side door and up the stairs, the safety and solitude of her room clutching her.

chapter eleven

The flight back from California was uneventful. During the Uber ride home, Jessica went over the events of the previous evening in her mind, worried that she had possibly missed something and had left evidence behind. Unfortunately, the screams had been her undoing and she had to get the hell out of there before she got pinched. It was a close enough call as it was.

Rather than try to get rid of any of the evidence while she was still in California, she stuffed the gloves into the pockets of her jeans and rolled her clothes up tightly, placing them in the dry-cleaning bag that the hotel had so graciously provided. She was thankful that the hotel was murderer-friendly.

Between the bag of clothes, her shoes and her old

laptop she retrieved, she placed them all inside her carryon luggage, determined to keep an eye on the evidence every step of the way. When she got home, she would get rid of the clothing—even the shoes. She couldn't be too careful regarding blood, hair, carpet fibers or any other evidence that hitchhiked out of Amanda Barrett's house.

Jessica's thoughts turned toward the laptop. How the hell had she left it behind? She had packed all of her personal items—or so she thought—and the Salvation Army had come and picked up anything left. Had she really been so careless as to leave it behind, letting it fall into the hands of a stranger? It seemed so coincidental that the person who purchased it was the mother of all Karen Carter fans, but stranger things existed. All Jessica knew was that she had to be more careful. Stupid mistakes such as that one would come back to haunt her if she didn't get her shit together.

Back in her apartment, she burned the gloves in a frying pan and took the melted remains, along with the clothing and shoes she had worn to the murder, and distributed them down all three garbage chutes around the building, the same as she had done with Lana Brook's body parts. If anyone came sniffing around, the evidence would be history by then.

The laptop was another issue. Jessica knew she had to get rid of it as not only did it have evidence of her transgressions, but it was now also a direct link back to Amanda Barrett. If the laptop was ever discovered, it would be game over for her. Karen Carter would be writing books from her prison cell.

At the bar counter, Jessica set the laptop down and opened it, powering it on in the process. The screen came to life. Jessica remembered it well as it was the computer she had used for a couple of years before taking over Lana's. She had never kept a password on it and it appeared that Amanda Barrett hadn't changed much, besides the desktop image.

As she browsed through the computer, she saw many new folders. One was labeled 'Jessica Nichols'. She clicked it. Hundreds of files popped up and as she read the titles, she realized that these were the files she had on it when she left it behind. She hadn't missed them, because she had copied the hard drive to transfer over to Lana's computer. Amanda had kept all Jessica's files on the laptop. She had to assume Amanda read all of them as well.

Covering her mouth with her trembling hand, Jessica realized how close she had come to being suspect number one. Had she left the laptop behind, the police would have processed it and found out everything they needed to know about her, Lana Brooks and the Karen Carter situation. She drew in a deep breath as she said a thank you in her head to nobody in particular.

Jessica started clicking open each of the file folders that didn't belong to her. Photos, spreadsheets, word documents and other files filled the folders, but at first glance, she didn't see anything too ominous that pertained to her.

Eventually, she found a folder labeled 'Karen Carter' and clicked it open. She opened the first document. A screenshot of what looked like the airline reservation she made to Tampa. The next screenshot was a shot of the Karen Carter manuscript she had been working on and judging from the time stamp on the photo, it was snapped about a month ago. The next photo was a shot of her logged into one of Lana's accounts.

Her phone buzzed and pulled her attention away from the computer. It was Ethan calling. She had texted him when she landed letting him know she was back in town. Jessica answered the phone.

"When did you get back?" Ethan asked.

"A couple of hours ago. How you been?"

"Good. Missing you a little bit though. God, that sounds strange coming out of my mouth."

"No kidding. It sounds strange hearing it."

"So how was Cali?"

"Uneventful," she lied.

"Care to give me all the details over dinner?"

Jessica smiled. "That can be arranged."

"Cool. I know this new place that I'm dying to eat at."

Jessica's throat clenched up at his choice of words and she had a small coughing fit.

"You okay?" he asked.

"Never better," she replied, recovering. "I could kill for a good steak right about now. I'm in."

They set up the time and Ethan gave her the address. After they ended the call, Jessica returned her attention to the laptop. As she clicked through the documents and files, she found many other screen-shots that Amanda had made as she watched Jessica doing things on Lana's computer, including shots of her logging into the accounts under her Jessica Nichols name. Amanda had enough to piece every-thing together.

Rubbing her eyes, Jessica tried to clear her head. If she hadn't covered her tracks well enough, detec-tives would start sniffing around soon. It was impor-tant that she get rid of the computer. If they came to talk with her, the only association she hoped they could prove was her presence in Orange at the time of the murder. Everything else would be circumstantial.

Clicking out of the folders, Jessica reached for the power button, but hesitated, noticing the Outlook icon on the taskbar at the bottom of the screen. She clicked, hoping Amanda's email might shed some light on who knew what. Had Amanda told anyone else?

Dozens of emails appeared and Jessica scrolled down the list. Most were junk mail messages. A few were confirmation emails regarding bills that were paid or products that had been ordered. An email from Delta Airlines caught her eye and she opened it. As she read through the email, she covered her mouth with her hand, a tightness forming in her chest.

The email was a plane ticket confirmation. The destination was New York and the date was in two days. Amanda Barrett had booked a trip to New York and Jessica knew in the pit of her stomach why. Flashes of her struggles with Lana Brooks shot through her mind as she wondered if Amanda had planned on coming to New York to do the same thing to her. Thankfully, that ticket would never be used.

Jessica powered off the computer and turned it over. From the kitchen junk drawer, she fished a small Phillips screwdriver. After removing the screws from the casing of the laptop, as well as the back, she unplugged the battery and removed the hard drive. In the kitchen, she filled up the sink with cold water and placed the laptop inside, letting it sit while she fixed herself a drink.

When the drink was gone, she fished the computer from the sink, dried it off the best she could and made a trip to the nearest trash chute, dumping the laptop down it, certain that it would end up in the city landfill in the next day or so.

After getting ready for her dinner date, Jessica ordered an Uber and when in the car, settled back in her seat. Her purse sat next to her and remembering, she reached inside, making sure the hard drive was still where she had placed it earlier. It was.

She turned to the driver. "How much extra to make a stop by Pier One?"

"It's not too far out of the way. I'm happy to stop there for free, as long as it's quick."

"That'd be great," she said, running her thumb over the cold, metal edge of the drive. "I just need to drop something off."

the karen carter series

BOOKS IN THE KAREN CARTER SERIES

Book One: One-Star Review
Book Two: Becoming Karen Carter
Book Three: A Review to Die For

about the author

R.E. Sargent is the author of three novels, four novelettes, and many short stories in the genres of suspense, supernatural, and horror. He is an active member of the Horror Writers Association, the Alliance of Independent Authors, and the Community of Literary Magazines and Presses. His short story, "Lucy," was featured in the 2021 Splatterpunk Award–nominated anthology *If I Die Before I Wake Volume 3 – Tales of Deadly Women and Retribution.*

R.E. lives in the Pacific Northwest with his wife and their Chocolate Lab. And the rain. Lots and lots of rain. He is thankful that writing is an indoor activity.

Correspondence to the author should be directed to any of the following:

facebook.com/r.e.sargentofficial

www.resargent.com

Made in United States
Troutdale, OR
08/13/2026

52329330R00073